The Very Beary Tooth Fairy

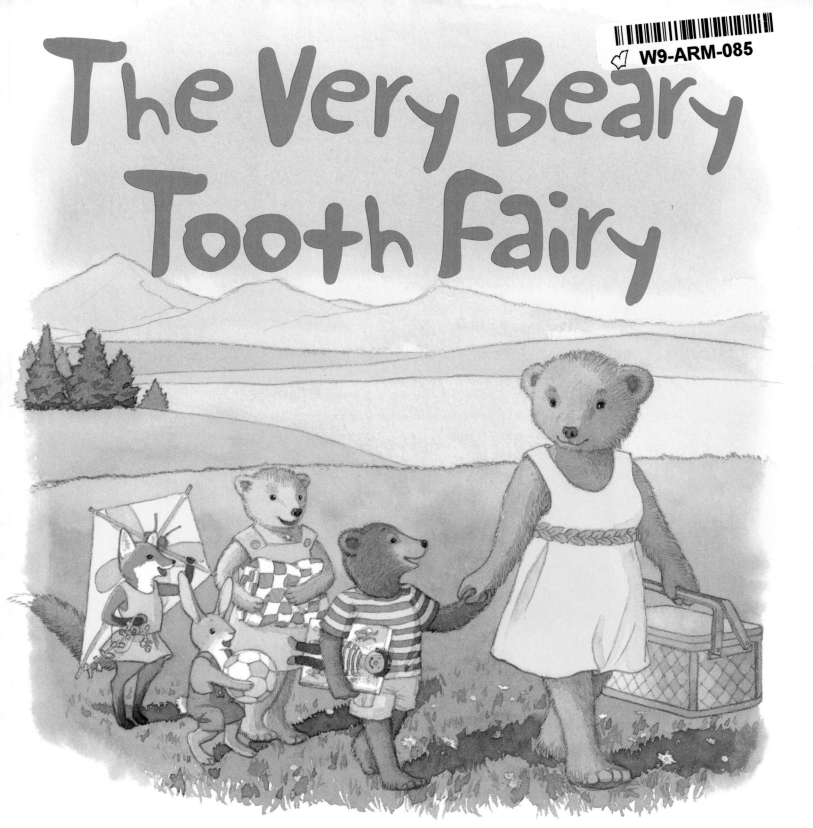

Arthur A. Levine • Illustrated by Sarah S. Brannen

SCHOLASTIC PRESS • NEW YORK

Library of Congress Cataloging-in-Publication Data

Levine, Arthur A., 1962-

The very beary tooth fairy / by Arthur A. Levine ; illustrated by Sarah S. Brannen. — 1st ed.   p.   cm.

Summary: Zach is a bear with a loose tooth, and he wants to know whether there is a tooth fairy just for bears.

ISBN 978-0-545-56238-6 — ISBN 978-0-439-47404-7   1. Tooth Fairy (Legendary character)—Juvenile fiction.

2. Bears—Juvenile fiction. [1. Tooth Fairy—Fiction. 2. Bears—Fiction.] I. Brannen, Sarah S., ill. II. Title.

PZ7.L57824Ver 2013   [E]—dc23   2012013798

10 9 8 7 6 5 4 3 2 1   13 14 15 16 17

Printed in the U.S.A. 40

First edition, February 2013

The text in this book was set in Minion Pro Regular.

The display type was set in Stanton ICG Regular.

The art in this book was done using watercolor and graphite

on 260 lb. Arches cold press watercolor paper.

Art direction and book design by Marijka Kostiw

For Sandy Koufax, Barack Obama, and every brave soul
who proved that "a bear can be anyone,
and anyone can be a bear."
— A. A. L.

For my mother, who has
always believed in me.
— S. S. B.

Zach's mom told him to stay away from people. "They are dangerous and unpredictable," she warned. And Zach did as he was told.

But one day he chased a bee across the field near his den
and wound up on the edge of a campsite.

Zach hid behind a rock and held his breath. Fortunately, the people were making a lot of noise and they hadn't noticed him.

"It feels weird!" said the boy, pushing his tongue against something in his mouth.

"Leave your tooth alone," said the boy's mother. "It will come out on its own. And then we can leave it under your pillow for the tooth fairy."

The boy got into the car, looking up at the high mountains, as if the tooth fairy might swoop down at any minute. His mother slammed her door shut and they drove off.

Zach touched his paw to his cheek. He too had a loose tooth, and now he had a question.

"Is the tooth fairy a bear or a person?" he asked his sister, Leah.

"Depends," she told him. Then she walked away with her pal Francine and wouldn't explain.

This was a problem. He was supposed to avoid people. What if the tooth fairy turned out to be one of them?

1. Tooth Fairy
2. Old Mother Hubbard
3. Santa Claus
4. Easter Bunny

Zach made a list and brought it to his friend Harrison.

"Well, the only one of those guys I know is the Easter Bunny: definitely a rabbit. I don't know about the tooth fairy," Harrison said. "What do you think?"

Zach shrugged and nudged his tooth with his tongue. Loose. Very loose. He had to figure it out soon.

Santa Claus was the only one he could cross off. Zach had stayed up late last Christmas to hear "Grr-ho-ho-ho" and found a note by the cookie plate with a bear-paw signature, clear as day.

That night Zach was so worried, he couldn't get to sleep.

"Mom," he said, "what can a bear be?"

"A bear can be anyone," she answered. "And anyone can be a bear."

She sounded very certain. But she always sounded that way.

Zach had bad dreams and woke up exhausted. All that day he was so afraid to lose his tooth that he wouldn't eat.

Leah romped into the den with Francine and a bag of candy

that some people had left behind at a campsite.

"Can we eat it, Mom?" she asked.

"Leah! What have I said about going near campsites?"

"There was no one there, I promise."

"Arrrrrr," growled their mother.

And she left the room.

Leah and Francine spread the candy out on the floor. Caramels.

"Mmmmmmm," said Francine, popping one in her mouth.

"MmmMMMM," said Leah.

"Can I have one?" Zach asked.

"Sure," said Leah, a little too sweetly. She knew what was coming.

Zach popped one in his mouth. He liked it. He cradled it first

on one side . . . then the other. Finally, he couldn't resist anymore

and he bit down.

"**AAAAAAA!**" Zach screamed and ran into his room, hiding under the covers. He refused to hear Leah's apology.

That night, Zach put the tooth as far away from his bed as he could. Then he huddled with one eye out of the covers, waiting to see what the tooth fairy would turn out to be.

And whether she would be dangerous. And unpredictable.

Soon enough, there was a scratching at his door and in came a bear wearing a crown of flowers and a tutu.

"I am the tooth fairy," sang the vision. "A very bear-y fairy, as you can see. And I am here with gifts for good little bears who have lost a tooth."

She leaned down and kissed
Zach lightly on the forehead. She
left an apple.

"Okay?" she asked.

Zach nodded.

He watched the triangle of
light fold shut as the tooth fairy
closed the door.

Then he settled back under
the covers and closed his eyes.